When I get bigger I'll be able to do lots of things.

WHEN I GET BIGGER

BY
MERCER MAYER

ALL THAT I CAN BE

BY MERCER MAYER

RANDOM HOUSE 🏠 NEW YORK

The material contained in this book was taken from the following publications: *When I Get Bigger* book, characters, text, and images © 1999 by Mercer Mayer, and *When I Grow Up* book, characters, text, and images © 1991 by Mercer Mayer.

Visit us on the Web!
randomhousekids.com
littlecritter.com
ISBN 978-0-399-55377-6
Printed in the United States of America
10 9 8 7 6 5 4 3 2 1

I'll go to the corner store by myself . . .

I'll wait until the light is green. Then I'll look both ways for cars before I cross the street.

I'll have my own watch
and I'll tell everyone
what time it is.

I'll go on a bus
to Grandma and
Grandpa's.

I'll go to first grade.

When I get bigger I'll have
a real leather football . . .

. . . my own radio, and a pair of
superpro roller skates.

I'll have a two-wheeler and a paper route.
I'll make lots of money.

At the playground
I'll help the little kids
on the swings.

I'll pick out
my own boots
at the shoe store.

I'll make a phone call
and dial it myself.

I'll order something from a catalog . . .

. . . and it will come in the mail.

When I get bigger I'll camp out
in the backyard all night long.

Or I'll stay up to
see the end of the
late movie.
Even if I get sleepy,
I won't go to bed.

But right now I have to go to bed . . .

. . . because Mom and Day say . . .

. . . I'm not bigger yet.

WHEN
I GROW UP

BY MERCER MAYER

When I grow up, I'll be a great dancer. I'll dance in the ballet.

But first I'll lead a long parade
through town.

Then I will join the circus.
I'll walk the tightrope and
everyone will cheer.

Or I might just be the
funniest clown in the world.

I will also teach lions and tigers
to dance and play music.

When I get tired of
being a circus star,
I'll be a mountain climber.

Then I will be a truck driver.
I will drive hundreds of miles
every day.

I will have a pet store, too.
All of the pets will be my friends,
and I will never sell any of them.

Just for fun, I will be
a world-famous doctor and
make everyone feel better.

I'll be a fire chief
and will rescue anyone
who needs rescuing.

I will be a police officer and help
everybody cross the street.

In my spare time, I will be a race-car driver. I will win every race.

If I get bored with that,
I will be a mail carrier
and deliver letters everywhere.

On the weekends, I will fly
an airplane. I will do dangerous
tricks in the air.

If I fall, I will just open my parachute
and float gently to the ground.

I will also be a very famous baker.
I'll make cakes and cookies.
No one will ever have to
eat liver or beans again.

Say, that reminds me,
I'm getting hungry.
"What's for dinner?" I ask.

"Liver and beans," Mom answers.

I can't wait until
I grow up!